Blue's Bad Dream

by Sarah Albee
illustrated by Ian Chernichaw

Simon Spotlight/Nick Jr.
New York   London   Toronto   Sydney

Based on the TV series *Blue's Clues*® created by Traci Paige Johnson,
Todd Kessler, and Angela C. Santomero as seen on Nick Jr.®

SIMON SPOTLIGHT
An imprint of Simon & Schuster Children's Publishing Division
1230 Avenue of the Americas, New York, New York 10020
© 2006 Viacom International Inc. All rights reserved. NICK JR., *Blue's Clues*, and all related titles, logos,
and characters are registered trademarks of Viacom International Inc. Created by Traci Paige Johnson,
Todd Kessler, and Angela C. Santomero.
All rights reserved, including the right of reproduction in whole or in part in any form.
SIMON SPOTLIGHT and colophon are registered trademarks of Simon & Schuster, Inc.
Manufactured in the United States of America
10 9 8 7 6 5 4 3 2
ISBN-13: 978-1-4169-1553-9
ISBN-10: 1-4169-1553-2

Blue was so excited! Her best friend, Magenta, was sleeping over.

"Good night, Blue!" said Magenta as she yawned and rolled over.

"Good night, Magenta!" said Blue, turning out the light.

Blue decided to read a storybook until she grew
sleepy. She looked at the pictures under the covers with a
flashlight so that she would not wake Magenta.

"This book is so exciting!" she whispered to herself.
It was a story about a fire-breathing dragon.

Blue stared at a picture of the dragon. The dragon had sharp claws and big teeth.

Blue turned the page quickly, then peeked at Magenta.
She was fast asleep. Blue closed the book and turned off
her flashlight. Soon she was fast asleep too.

Blue started to dream. She dreamed about the dragon from her book.

"Roarrr!" he growled, showing his sharp claws.

In her dream Blue tried to run away from the scary dragon.

"Blue!" said a voice. "Wake up! You're having a bad dream!"

Blue opened her eyes and saw Magenta leaning over her. The dragon was gone.

Blue's heart was thumping in her chest.

"I dreamed about a scary dragon," said Blue. "It had sharp-looking claws!"

"Oooh," said Magenta. "That does sound scary! Let's go get something to drink. That might help."

Blue and Magenta got out of bed and went to the kitchen.

"Hello, Magenta. Hello, Blue," said Mrs. Pepper. "Why are you still awake?"

Blue told Mr. Salt and Mrs. Pepper about her bad dream.

"No wonder you felt scared!" said Mrs. Pepper kindly. "Remember, Blue, that the dragon in your dream is not real. But it shows what a great imagination you have!"

"Have some warm milk," said Mr. Salt. "It will help you get back to sleep and dream nice dreams."

Blue and Magenta drank their milk. Blue already felt better.

Mr. Salt and Mrs. Pepper brought Blue and Magenta back to Blue's room.

"Is this the dragon you dreamed about?" asked Mr. Salt, looking at the book near Blue's bed.

Blue nodded.

"We know a story about a *nice* dragon," said Mrs. Pepper. "Why don't we tell it to you?"

Blue and Magenta snuggled up under their covers to listen.

Tickety listened too.

Mr. Salt and Mrs. Pepper told them a story about a friendly dragon. This dragon loved to play games and fly loop-de-loops around the clouds.

After the story Mr. Salt and Mrs. Pepper turned on a night-light. Then they said good night to Blue and Magenta.

"Remember," said Mr. Salt softly, "dreams are just your imagination."

"Does that mean Blue can dream about nice dragons?" Tickety asked.

Blue nodded sleepily. "There might be dream dragons that are really nice," she murmured.

After a short time Blue and Magenta fell asleep. Tickety Tock counted sheep until she fell asleep too. Soon the whole house was sleeping peacefully.

Blue dreamed about the dragon again!

"Roarrr!" the dragon growled, showing his sharp claws.

But this time Blue was not afraid. "I'm Blue," she said to the dragon.

"I'm Ralph," said the dragon. Ralph smiled at Blue, showing her lots and lots of pointy teeth.

"You're a nice dragon!" said Blue.

"Yes," said Ralph. "Roaring and showing my claws is just my way of saying hello."

"Do you know any games we can play?" asked Ralph. Blue smiled. "Sure. I know a great game. It's called Blue's Clues."

The two of them played Blue's Clues and then flew loop-de-loops around the clouds. Then they had juice and muffins. Blue kept hoping her dream would never end . . . but suddenly it did. Blue heard birds tweeting, and then the dragon started to fade away. "Good-bye, Ralph!" Blue called.

Blue opened her eyes. Birds were tweeting. The sun was shining. It was morning! Blue smiled at her friend.

"Wake up, Magenta!" she said. "I had a dream about a dragon!"

"Another dragon?" asked Magenta. "Was it scary?"
"No, it was great!" said Blue. "We played Blue's Clues,
and we flew around the clouds, and we had juice and . . ."

Just then a delicious smell filled Blue's room.

"Muffins!" said Blue. "Let's go eat the muffins Mr. Salt and Mrs. Pepper made!"

And the two friends did just that.